Dear Parents,

The easy-to-read books in this series are based on The Puzzle Place™, public television's highly praised new show for children that teaches not ABC's or 123's, but "human being" lessons!

In these books, your child will learn about getting along with children from all different backgrounds, about dealing with problems, and making decisions—even when the best thing to do is not always so clear.

Filled with humor, the stories are about situations which all kids face. And best of all, kids can read them all on their own, building a sense of independence and pride.

So come along to the place where it all happens. Come along to The Puzzle Place™....

Copyright © 1996 Lancit Copyright Corporation/KCET. All rights reserved. Published by Grosset & Dunlap, Inc., a member of The Putnam & Grosset Group, New York. GROSSET & DUNLAP is a trademark of Grosset & Dunlap, Inc. THE PUZZLE PLACE and THE PUZZLE PLACE logo are trademarks of Lancit Media Productions, Ltd. and KCET. Published simultaneously in Canada. Printed in the U.S.A. Library of Congress Catalog Card Number: 95-62119   ISBN 0-448-41285-3   A B C D E F G H I J

The Puzzle Place is a co-production of Lancit Media Productions, Ltd., and KCET/Los Angeles. Major funding provided by the Corporation for Public Broadcasting and SCEcorp.

BEN'S GLASSES

By David Johnson

Illustrated by Matthew Fox

Based on the teleplay, "Picture Perfect,"
by Ellis Weiner and Jennifer Bross

GROSSET & DUNLAP · NEW YORK

Ben wears glasses.
He wears glasses
so he can see better.

He wears glasses
every day —
to watch TV...

to pitch hay...

...and to take care of
the animals
on his farm.

But today is picture day
at The Puzzle Place.
Ben wants to look his best.
It's time to get ready.

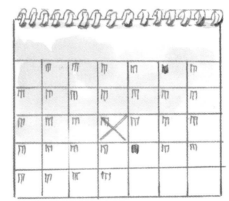

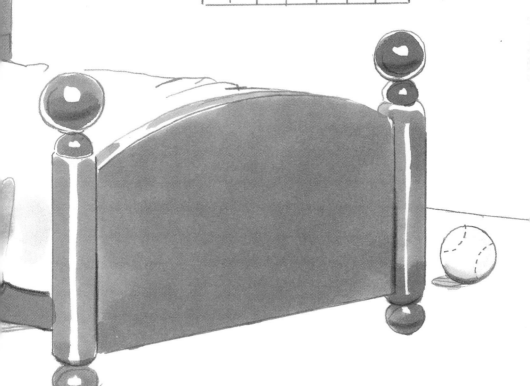

He puts on
his best shirt.

He brushes his hair.

"I look goofy
in these glasses,"
says Ben.
So he takes them off.

Then off he goes
to The Puzzle Place.
"Hi, Jody!" says Ben
to a hat rack.

"I am over here,"
says Jody.
She gives Ben
a funny look.

"Your hair looks
different today, Kiki,"
says Ben.

"Silly Benny!" Kiki says.

"That is not me.

That is a mop."

"Oh," says Ben.

"So it is."

Then he goes

into the bathroom.

The girls' bathroom.

"Oops!"

"Eek!" yells Julie.

She runs out

of the bathroom.

Ben comes out
of the bathroom.
He bumps into a chair.
"Excuse me,"
Ben says to the chair.

"What is the matter
with Ben today?"
Kiki asks Julie.

"Ben does not look
like Ben.
Ben does not act
like Ben."

"Oh, now I know
what is the matter!"
says Kiki.
"Where are your
glasses, Benny?"

"I look goofy in glasses,"
says Ben.

"You look good in glasses,"
says Kiki.
"You look goofy
when you talk
to mops and chairs!"

"But glasses make me
...different,"
says Ben.

"We are all different,"
says Kiki.
"Different hair!
Different color skin!
Different in lots of ways!"

Ben puts on his glasses.

"You are right,"

says Ben.

"I can see that now!"

And what else
can Ben see?
Ben can see that
it is picture time.

And Ben can see…

...that the camera
is upside down!

So the cameraman
holds the camera
the right way.
Then they all say…

...CHEESE!